TEENS UNFILTERED

A Literary Anthology

EDITED BY:

DAKOTA WACKWITZ

Wild Ink Publishing
wild-ink-publishing.com

ISBN: 978-1-964885-36-0

Dear Reader,

Welcome to *Teens Unfiltered*, a collection of raw, real, and remarkable voices. The following pages are filled with short stories and poetry that capture the messy, beautiful, and sometimes surprising world through the eyes of teens. Read at your own peril! No filters. No apologies. Just truth told in ways that will make you laugh, think, and maybe even see things differently. Every piece here was written by young writers who dared to share their stories. Some will tug at your heart. Others might spark an idea or a memory. All of them prove that words have power. By holding this book, you're also supporting something bigger. All proceeds go to the Young Writers Workshop Scholarship Fund at Messiah University, helping more teens find their voices and tell their stories. Thank you, dear reader, for being part of this mission. Now, dive in. Let these words surprise you. Let them challenge you. Most of all, let them remind you that no matter who you are, your story matters too.

Happy reading,

Abigail Wild

Founder, Wild Ink Publishing

Table of Contents

Cyborg
by Lara Chamoun

The Magic Keeper
by Mabel May

Creek Summers
by Maura Pensinger

The Woman Behind The Glass
by Honora Quinn

Forevermore
by Brendan Sack

Question
by Karly Gerow

Too Late
by Karly Gerow

Escapade of a Quasi-Hero
by Brendan Sack

As You Are in Your Bedroom in 2024, 2:56am
by Lara Chamoun

Alive to Speak It
by Lara Chamoun

Being Used is Like Being a Trash Can
by Karly Gerow

Scare Town
by Kiki Hawkins

The Unrighteous Raccoon
by Brendan Sack

Rumpelstiltskin
by Karly Gerow

Namb the Preamble
by Noel N. Moira

West Coast
by Karly Gerow

Dear Dad,
by Karly Gerow

What Am I?
by Skai de Leon

Cyborg

by Lara Chamoun

The Watcher remembers the windy Tuesday morning when the first part was replaced. It was certainly not a significant one—a knuckle joint that had started to ache in the breeze. The draft would stop where there seemed to be an unnecessary gap in between bone and ligament. It caused The Watcher much discomfort whenever they knocked on doors or made fists. The doctor offered a quick and painless solution. It was just a click of metal where there was once bone.

The bone, of course, was tossed in a sterile, orange biohazard bin. That was the brief moment when The Watcher's breath stumbled on a tightrope: the cold that hit when a singular warmth was removed. The doctor's hands were practiced, precise as they made the incision. There was no pain, just a chill and a tear-track of red that The Watcher could almost taste dripping onto the white floor. They often bite their tongue.

The Watcher stepped outside, and the wind parted around their knuckle like water flowing around stones. They forgot that weakness and read somewhere that the isotope Plutonium-239 can take up to 24,1000 years longer than human flesh to decompose. The Watcher hasn't visited a natural history museum in years, so they forget about paleopathologists and archeologists.

The replacements don't stop there, of course. There is a knee that acts up during the rainy season and a shoulder blade that feels strange under the sun. There are many beneficial upgrades available, says the doctor. Upgrades for upgrades for upgrades. Did you know Tungsten is denser than Plutonium? The Watcher floats a bit because they no longer have to bear the weight of joints giving way or muscles against gravity or that grief-shaped pebble on their tongue. That's long gone. The metal in The Watcher's mouth no longer tastes of much. At least the landmarks cut into their tongue are gone; they were memory-shaped and hurt to eat with.

And then The Watcher had the big scar covered with a polished titanium plate. The difference in texture between the jagged, raised edges and smooth mirror-metal bothered them. They wanted to be able to smile at themself in the reflection of new, unhurt skin.

The Magic Keeper

by Mabel May

Everyone knows who I am, but not in the way people may think. My name is Kaitlin, and I'm your typical sophomore girl at East Claw High School. I'm a straight-A student, writer, and social outcast. I'm the target of every bully at school, and they don't fail to show me that. I constantly get picked on like I'm easy pickings. I made it very easy for them all, I never really fought back. But that all changed one weekend when my writing became my everyday reality.

Chapter One

It was finally the last class of the day, and I was oh so more than ready to get home. All I wanted to do was curl up in my hammock chair with Cinder my bearded dragon, with a soft blanket, a cup of blueberry tea, and write my latest idea for a story in my notebook. Writing with Cinder was my happy place, my second home.

Writing didn't ever feel like writing to me. It felt as though I was looking through someone else's eyes into a world I longed to be in. Writing felt right—not like a side job or a chore, but a joy that could only be described as a feeling of home and belonging.

There are no wrong answers when it comes to imagination. Only endless possibilities with a new adventure around every corner just waiting to be written.

* * *

I was snapped from my thoughts as the last bell rang, signaling the end of the school day. I stood pushing the chair back behind me as my hands flew to my belongings scattered on the desk in front of me. I quickly rushed to push and cram everything into my backpack trying to make it out of the class and school so my idea wouldn't leave my brain like rain free falling from clouds on a new spring day.

As I finished zipping the main pocket of my bag, I sidestepped toward the door, twisting my whole body in the process. My right hand still held one of the backpack straps, so I forcefully yanked it off the desk as I speed-walked toward the door, throwing it over and onto my shoulder.

I ran out the door throwing a "Have a good weekend!" over my shoulder to my English teacher who still sat at her desk with her oversized oval glasses practically falling off the bridge of her nose. I couldn't help but chuckle at that as I continued through the door and into the bustling hallway. Elbow to elbow as usual. I was very uncomfortable; I always was when life called me to be this close to any other human being.

Finally, I arrived at the main hallway and noticed the exit door visible just around the corner. I let out a sigh of relief as most of the people in the hallway went in other directions or had already left considering I had been in the back.

As I rounded the corner the only thing on my mind was the distance between me and my creativity.

Smiling to myself, I ran right into something. It was a person. Off balance, I fell on my butt making my backpack fly off my back and onto the floor in the process. Before I could even say or do anything, a laugh that reeked of evil intentions sounded in front of me.

I looked up to see Carla, a senior known not to be trifled with at East Claw High. Who, just my luck, was glowering down at me.

"Going somewhere? *Freak.*" She elongated the word freak. She was basically hissing the word as she flipped her long, newly dyed blond hair over her left shoulder with a wicked grin.

"Um, yes. home." I tried to act as if I wasn't affected by her

but it was impossible seeing that I was on the floor and she and all her lackeys were crowded around me.

"Well, why don't you stay a while." Carla took one long glance at my bag, and I knew I was not getting home as soon as I wanted to.

"Brodie, Austin. You know what I'm going to ask." Two short look a likes, I'm assuming twins, walked up from behind Carla and the rest of her minions. Before I could do anything, one of them grabbed my backpack, taking the one thing I never let anyone have a chance to get close to: my notebook. And the other one had their open water bottle in hand.

I quickly got up and tried to reach my notebook before any damage could come to it. But Carla whispered something more to her blind followers who then stepped in front of me, blocking my path but not my view. My face paled as I watched the two short boys who Carla had called Brodie and Austin discard my bag which clattered to the floor, and mockingly held out my notebook holding the water bottle now open over it. No water spilled but it was enough to scare me.

"Wait! Please don't." I desperately tried to push past Carla's brainwashed army that stood between me and my stories and the only thing that made me feel like I had a place in the world. But to my dismay, Carla's lackeys were stronger than me all put together and easily kept me in front of them, and farther away from my life's work.

"Why? Surely you don't care that much about school work. Do you? You can just buy another notebook." Carla moved to stand behind me, so I turned to her. That way, I didn't have to look at my stories and characters, my only sense of home being destroyed. "No. No it's not school work it's—" I covered my mouth with my hands. I instantly regretted my words.

A look of pure wicked delight crossed over Carla's face as she crossed her arms.

"Oh? Is that the little notebook you're always writing your silly story in? I didn't recognize it." I could tell that those words were a pure lie. She knew exactly what she was doing. She made a circular motion with her hand towards her minions behind me.

Less than a second later, strong hands seized my shoulders and turned me around. I tried to pull myself from the person's grip but they held firm. All I could do was watch as I was engulfed in sorrow, anger, and remorse. I could feel hot tears spilling from my eyes and down my cheeks, as I watched Brodie and Austin holding my notebook open, all while pouring water on its pages, destroying all I had made and built over the years. Carla and all her flunkies all laughed and finally released their hold on my shoulders. Leaving me to fall to my knees before my destroyed heart, in a puddle of defeat.

I stood after a moment and wiped my tears. I looked around for a second and my eyes fell on my backpack. I walked over and picked it up, throwing it over my shoulder again. As I did so, I turned to where my notebook, my portal to happiness and joy, was now a pile of mush. I walked over to it then, slowly bent down and picked up the remains of what was left. I walked over to the bin with a sense of sorrow. It hurt me and my soul to throw it away. But as I did, I made a vow to myself and any of my future stories or characters. I was not going to let Carla or anyone else at this stupid school walk all over me. I had always stayed quiet, but I was done being a target.

Chapter Two

I walked into my house and was greeted with the smell of hot blueberry tea. Which was somewhat calming.

"Hey, mom! I'm home!" I closed the door and then stopped advancing by the archway that led into the living room and kitchen, where I saw my mom set a cup of what I was assuming was the blueberry tea I was smelling.

I kicked off my tennis shoes and dropped my backpack on the floor near the front door.

"Hey, Kaitlin! I made you some tea. Wow, what happened? You look like you were crying." My mom sat at the island in the middle of the kitchen: her and her stupid mom telekinesis. I grabbed the cup and took a long-awaited sip of the warm and welcoming taste.

"I'm fine Mom. I just—" I paused thinking of what to say that she would buy. "I just yawned a second ago which caused tears in my eyes." Nice going genius. What's the best you could come up with?

I smiled at her and turned towards the stairwell that would lead up to where I wanted to curl up and die.

* * *

I creaked open the door to my room and sighed at the familiar homey smell that wafted my way as I stepped inside. I closed the door behind me and just stayed standing there for a second, looking around.

Near my window that faced the front yard was a hammock chair that hung from the ceiling with tassels dangling from every side. Near that, covering every other wall was floor to ceiling white bookshelves overflowing with fantasy book after fantasy book.

Covering the floor in the dead center was a purple fluffy rug that was circle shaped. For some reason, I had picked that over a real rug when we moved here.

On the opposite wall, farthest from the window and closest to the door was my bed. It was a queen-sized white banister bed that had a blanket spread across it that I had crocheted a few years back with a mix of purples and blues. And my decorative three layers of pillows that matched the rug in pinkish purples as well. On the right, there were posters over my pine desk with a bulletin board for all my *freakish* ideas.

Lastly, on the left was my old dresser that my poppa had made before he had died years and years ago. My eyes landed on the glass enclosure for the little bundle of joy that was currently scurrying around excitingly—Cinder, my bearded dragon. On the ceiling, right where the wall and roof began to meet, were my fairy lights and fake ivy hanging all along the top. On the ceiling itself were glow in the dark stars that when exposed to light, after a while, you could turn off the lights and they would glow. Ever since I had read a book with a character who could control night I fell in love with the way stars looked.

I set my tea on my very Victorian-era pine nightstand and walked over to where Cinder had his tongue out of his mouth and gawking, which was a sign he was happy. He kept stepping to the side a few steps when the glass would fog near his snout.

I couldn't help but laugh when I opened his enclosure to see him jumping up in down, He was clearly excited I was home.

"Hey Cinder, buddy. You ready to get out of there?" I lowered one of my hands into his glass enclosure and Cinder didn't hesitate to jump into my palm licking my hand. I lifted my hand from the enclosure and Cinder crawled up the sleeve of my pleated tuxedo shirt, to sit upon my shoulder.

I walked over to my desk and opened a drawer, pulling out a new notebook and pen. As I sat in my overly soft hammock chair, Cinder nuzzled my neck, as if to say I'm sorry for what happened. So I patted him on the head and opened the note book to begin, hopefully, somewhat salvaging what I could remember about what I had already written.

Chapter three

I had no idea how long I had been sitting in that hammock chair, but as I looked up from my note book to gaze out the window, I noticed it was dark. I checked my alarm clock which sat on my night stand. The clock read seven thirty in its obnoxious red bold letters. I looked on my right shoulder to see Cinder fast asleep in the crook of my neck. I slowly stood trying not to wake him and sat my note book on to my desk. I slowly walked over to Cinder's enclosure and carefully and as gently as I could, I picked him up to lay in my palms and lowered him onto his favorite log, right under the heating lamp.

To my utmost shock, he just flipped onto his back and continued his slumber. I chuckled and as I watched him. After a minute I put the top of his enclosure back on and snapped it back in to place.

I turned to where my pj's had been discarded that morning on the floor near the bathroom door. I picked them up and turned the knob of the bathroom door open.

When I walked inside, I closed and locked the door behind me, setting my pj's down on the counter next to the sink. I looked at myself in the mirror, my hands were covered in pen marks. As I took my long brown wavy hair down from my high pony tail, I saw them looking almost like scabs. I set my pony tail holder off to the side and began to undress, turning on the hot water in the shower.

After a moment of letting the water heat, I stepped over the tub and as I positioned myself to stand directly under the water, it made my skin fuzzy and warm, like winter switching to spring. I closed my eyes and just let the hot water flow off my scalp, my eyes, and then my body, sending me into a sense of calm.

After I got out of the shower and was in my pj's, I slipped on my fuzzy pink bunny slippers to match the pink cotton pajamas. I plopped down onto my bed and slid under the covers. I twisted my body to get closer to the lamp that sat on the short night stand next to my bed.

I reached out and pulled the string, turning the last source of light off, besides my bright red alarm clock. When I lay flat on my back I glanced across the room to see it. The clock now read eight ten. I turned my head back to look up at the ceiling, gazing at the glow in the dark stars. I blinked a few times, fighting off sleep. But after a second, I let the comforting feel of my sheets and covers of weighted blankets and quilt weigh me down into sleep. But as I did fall asleep, I could have sworn I saw a glimpse of something bright. Not like a flashlight, but something moving itself, as if it were alive.

But unfortunately, I didn't have a chance to investigate further. Because my eyes closed, and my mind drifted into the solitude of my dreams.

* * *

It was odd; I was walking through what looked to be any old forest. But as I continued to walk, small glowing orbs of light appeared. They swirled around me for a second, then lit up a path that I assumed they wanted me to follow. They lined up going in the direction they wanted me to go. I couldn't help but wonder where they were taking me.

As I reached a clearing, I could see through the underbrush a bigger orb of light. I don't know why but I felt drawn to it, as if I knew it, like I would a person.

"Hello, Kaitlin dear." The orb spoke, flickering with every word.

Shocked, I stayed where I was.

"Who—What are you?" I asked, still in the brush, my limbs refusing to budge.

"Come now, young one. I promise you; I am no threat. I am in fact a friend." The orb said, floating a bit closer. For some reason I did not cower, I obeyed and came out from my hiding spot. As I stepped into the clearing, I couldn't help my small smile. For a change something wasn't picking on me. It felt nice to be seen and not walked over.

"What are you?" I asked again, my voice a bit more steady this time.

"I am a guide, here to help you." The orb's light seemed to glow brighter as I didn't move away and only seemed to be more curious.

"Why do I need a guide?" I was now closer to it, looking at it all over to absorb some of the wonder I was feeling.

"That question will be answered in time. But I need to know something first." I know the orb didn't have a face, but if it did, I could just picture it smiling wide at me. The orb sounded kind and goodhearted, its female voice warm like a summer breeze. "You are a creator, a writer, yes?" The orb's question caught me off guard, and my eyes widened slightly.

"Y—yes. How do you know that?" I asked, my voice showing my shock.

"I know a lot of things about you, Kaitlin. Things you have yet to discover about yourself, and things you already know. I know a lot about all things, actually." The orb said, her voice softening slightly.

I was absolutely stunned, but before I could ask the million questions whirling in my head, the orb spoke again, her voice sounding more hurried now.

"Kaitlin, you—" Before she could finish, my vision faded to black once more and the distant sounds of my alarm clock going off were the only thing I could hear. It was almost as if half of me was still encapsulated by the beautiful, enchanted forest I had just left behind.

Chapter four

It was Saturday afternoon, and a pleasant one at that. I love the weekends. They give me a chance to let my brain have a break, yes. But they also give me a chance to relax with Cinder. And anyone who knows me knows I don't relax. I'm either doing one thing or another, I hardly sit still, and I never ever just sit inside and do nothing. I'm always doing something important—well, that's important to me.

Cinder and I were currently outside, and I was propped up against the giant maple tree in my backyard that overlooked the river below the hill. We were surrounded by a pile of books and of course, I had my notebook and pen in hand. The sun was casting rays of light, warming my skin and shining light onto my empty pit of thoughts.

Cinder was running over my legs and around them and jumping. I chuckled as I watched him, he was having the time of his life. Cinder loved the outdoors, constantly rubbing his belly on blades of grass or crawling on my arm.

I continued to watch the river below run along the banks and saw the occasional bob of an otter or log. Out of the corner of my eye, I saw a light appear to my right. Not the sun, I knew that. I turned to look, and it was the same ball of light I had seen in my dream last night. I sat up straighter, and Cinder went flying off my shoulder and onto my lap with a squeak.

"Do not be afraid, for I am—" Before the woman trapped inside the ball of light could finish. I spoke, my words spilling out in one quick breath.

"You're the thing from my dream!" I slowly stood, pushing my back against the oak tree's rough bark. Cinder ran behind the only space left between my ankle and the high, uneven roots.

"Yes child, it is me. I don't believe we got to finish our interrupted conversation." The ball of light flew a little closer to me and Cinder, and I, for whatever reason, felt welcome and safe. My body, to my surprise, relaxed.

"So last night wasn't a dream, you were real. Why do you seem so familiar?" I took a step closer and felt a new added weight on my ankle. Cinder was crawling up my leg. I bent down to pick him up and put him on my shoulder, as the ball of light's gentle female voice answered.

"Strong bond between the two of you. I can see he sees you as his sister." I was surprised to hear this. Cinder was my best friend, and yet this thing was saying he saw me as a sister. It warmed my heart, filling it with pride.

"It's a good thing, to have pets—companions to stick with you through anything. The bond between you two is admirable. It's strong." I smiled and glanced at my shoulder where Cinder looked into my eyes with his adorable black voids.

"Anyway," the voice cleared her throat then continued. "I am here to talk about something important."

* * *

After a few minutes, the light had fully explained. She could give me a chance at a better life.

"So? Do you want to be welcomed at a place somewhere you know?" I was hesitant for a moment. I had no idea what she meant by *somewhere I know*? The only place I knew was Salt Lake City. I was born and raised in this house, this town, this area in general. I had never gone anywhere else. Nonetheless, I looked at the light and nodded.

"Yes. I—I want to leave. I want to stop feeling like a nobody. I want to be someone important, for once in my life." The light, even though she had no face or emotions, seemed pleased by my answer.

"Are you ready?" I was taken aback—we were leaving now? What about all my things, and belongings?

"Wait. We're leaving now? What about my life here?" I don't know why I was concerned or even cared. As far as everyone else knew in this town, I didn't exist.

"Oh, don't worry. Your human things will not be needed where we are going. And before you ask, yes. Your little lizard friend is going with you." I was a little confused. If I was moving somewhere wasn't I going to need my stuff?

"Step forward, child, and place your hand on me. It may tingle, but do not pull away." I did exactly that without thinking. It was as if my limbs knew what to do before I even did. As I took a few steps toward the orb, I held out my right hand and slowly placed it on the surface of the light. It sent a shiver down my spine. Not of pain, but of recognition. Like I was supposed to do this. Like I knew this thing, but just hadn't seen it in a long time, like a family reuniting after a decade.

"Hold on tight, young one. Oh, and you might want to hold on to your friend there, too." Without a second thought, I moved my free hand to hold Cinder tightly to my chest.

With a blink of an eye, the ball of light started to glow brighter than the sun. I didn't dare pull my hand away, afraid of what it could do to me and Cinder. I squeezed my eyes shut, enough to where it caused slight strain in my eyes to do so.

After what felt like not even a second, the ball of light spoke again. The light dimmed to its natural glow.

"You can look now child, welcome home, Phoenix." As I opened my eyes, I noticed we weren't in my backyard any longer.

We were in a clearing of the same woods from my dream where I had first met the light.

I turned to ask where we were and noticed my hand that was still stretched out. My fingertips were now golden, claw-like endings, that looked to be about an inch long. My hands had been turned black with ash, growing lighter in color the higher it got, finally stopping at my wrists. My fingers were the darkest of black, my wrist a grayish color. I let my eyes travel up my arm, and I noticed I was no longer wearing my purple tank top. Instead, a wine-red dress that went nearly to the ground but stopped at my ankles. It was a dress with no sleeves that wrapped around my neck, with strands of fabric loose that added elegance to the dress. My chest was covered despite the low cut, which I was fine with, and it gave me a sense of mystery and elegance.

"What the—" Before I could even finish, I heard something next to me on the ground. It sounded like a sneeze. I looked down to see a tiny arm-length dragon curled up on the ground. Its underbelly was dandelion yellow, while its top was midnight black.

"Cinder?! Is that you?!" I bent down, and sure enough, the little being's black eyes confirmed that it was indeed Cinder.

Out of the corner of my eye, I saw the ripples of water. I turned to see a lake as blue as the sky itself. I leaned forward to see my reflection, and I froze in shock. My outfit and cool new hands weren't the only thing that had changed.

My eyes were no longer my hazel brown-green, but they were a bright yellow with a black slit down the middle. Almost like a dragon's—no, exactly like a dragon's. My hair was no longer in its messy bun; my long wavy brown hair was down and falling just below my shoulder blades. In my mouth, my canines were sharper, and pointy on both top and bottom. My ears were no longer rounded like a human's but were pointy as a Fae's. But the thing that shocked me the most was atop my head sat two pairs of golden horns. Two golden ram horns were curled on the side of my head, along with two on the very top of my head. These were thinner and taller than the others, pointing upward towards the sky.

I continued to look at my reflection in shock until I finally realized what I was. I was no longer in the human world, and I certainly was no longer a human myself, either. I was in the world of magic, and as for me, I was now a Fae.

Chapter five

From behind me, I heard the light move forward, coming closer. "Where are we? What happened to Cinder?" I had a million questions swirling in my head, begging to be answered. "Surely you recognize this place and what you are. You created it, Phoenix." I looked away from the clear-as-a-mirror reflection, and back at the light.

"What?" I was so confused; the only world I created was… Elanor.

"Wait. You mean to tell me that this place is… Elanor?" I looked around the forest clearing at the midnight lilies that sprouted here and there. At the tree's bark that had a slight gray hue, with leaves as blue as the evening sky.

I then looked back at my reflection in the water. She was right, I looked just like the mystics in the…

"This is the Melder grove, from my book, Isn't it?" I turned my head to look back at the light, as the dots started to connect in my mind.

"Yes Phoenix, I brought you home. You may have been born in the human world, But your heart and soul belong here: with your friends and home you created." I looked back up at the light, which was now right behind me.

"Phoenix? My name is Kaitlin." The ball of light laughed, her warm female voice echoing off the trees around us in the clearing.

"Oh, sweet child. Here among your sisters and brothers, you no longer have your human name. You are Fae, Phoenix, Protector Of The Wood And Wielder Of Fire." For some reason, a sense of pride filled me. I was in the world I created, and I was proud of it. I was no longer a weak human; I had powers. Fire, apparently. I had been given another chance, and I wasn't going to let anyone here walk all over me like I had in the human world. I belonged here and as long as I had Cinder, I was going to be more than perfect.

* * *

After the ball of light had explained everything, she started to float away, saying her work here was done.

"Wait, I never got your name. Who are you?" Cinder wrapped around my neck and lifted his head to watch.

"Who I am isn't important, Phoenix. You will learn my name in time, child. For now, you have a new life to live. Make the most of it." And with that, she disappeared, evaporating into thin air.

I just stood there looking at everything I had created around me. My world, my home.

As I was lost in thought, I heard bushes rustle behind me. I turned, getting low to the ground, and bared my new fangs. I conjured a fireball in each hand, ready to defend myself and Cinder, who was still wrapped around my neck. Instead of a threat, two girls who were also Fae, walked out with their hands up. The one on the left had pale skin with the lightest undertone of gray. Her hair was long and white, with braids over her ear fins that fell below her shoulder blades. Her eyes were light blue like the lake to my right. Her fingers were webbed between, including her thumb. She didn't seem all that aggressive and looked kind, almost like an innocent child.

The one on the right showed no identifiable emotion. Her chocolate brown face was solemn, as I watched her eyes rake me up and down, assessing my new Fae form. I wondered if they knew if I was new to this world. My world. The girl's dark grass-green hair was in a half up, half down, hairstyle. The front strands were in two small braids leading to the back of her head, then flowed with the rest of the shoulder length, wavy hair. Fastened into the two small braids were white flowers with gold centers. Not daisies, but a river lily. I had written about them a few years ago, and completely forgotten I had. She had gold marks in rings around her arms, and her lips had one vertical line of gold to match. I noticed that on her fingers, there were symbols in the language I made up for this world, too. It translated to 'Plant Wielder.' She had a dress of green; the dress was the same color as rich green as her hair, and it fell to her lower calves. Her eyes were also a cold, calculating, rich green that seemed to stare into my soul.

I shook my head to silence myself out of my thoughts. "Who are you?" I was shocked by how cold my voice sounded when I spoke. It seemed to shock the two Fae in front of me too, because they both shifted their stances. The one on the right, the so called 'Plant Wielder,' stepped forward.

"We are the protectors of this wood. Who are you? And why are you in our forest?" I stood to my full new height, making my fire disappear.

"Who's the cutie on your neck?" The one who looked like a walking fish spoke up, pointing to Cinder. I was right, she seemed not be able to hurt a fly.

"This is Cinder my bear—I mean dragon, Cinder. And I am Phoenix, Wielder Of Fire. And I'm here because… well, because

I have nowhere else to go. Now, answer my questions. Who are both of you?" The two Fae looked at each other as if communicating silently. After a few seconds, they both nodded and turned back to me. The one with river lilies took another step forward, her face softer now.

"I am Clover, a plant Fae." Then the fish one stepped forward with a wide smile. "And I am Lotus, a water Fae. You said you have nowhere to go, yes?" I relaxed a bit, then shifted Cinder to curl around my left arm.

"Yes, you could say I…" I paused, petting Cinder, trying to think of what to say that wouldn't sound absolutely ridiculous. "I'm not very welcome where I'm from. They see me as different. So, I left." Both their facial expressions crossed with knowing, as if what I said hit a nerve that both of them knew all too well. "Well, Clover… I think we found ourselves a big sister." I guess I looked more surprised than I felt after Lotus said that, because Clover chuckled, which surprised me more. I thought she was a stony, emotionless Fae. Clover just walked over to me with a soft smile and held out her hand.

"Well, sis? Are you ready to join our cause to protect this forest?" I just stared at her hand and felt my eyes burn, threatening to let tears fall. She kept her hand out for me to take, and she didn't pull away. I looked up at her, and she was smiling. I took her hand, and we shook. Lotus squealed and ran to us both, pulling us into a group bear hug.

"Welcome, Sister!" For such a kind and small thing, she had the grip of a crab's pinchers.

After she let us go, they both motioned me to follow. I looked at Cinder, who looked as happy as I felt.

That female light was right: I was unwelcome and unappreciated in the human world. My gifts and creativity were overlooked, but here, I had a family who knew what it was like to be an outcast. I had little sisters, and I had a home. I had a purpose, more than scribbling in a notebook my whole life. Now, I was powerful. I was going to learn and explore this world that was mine since the first day I picked a note book. If I ran into Belladonna, Bastian, and Artemis, I would help them, because as their creator, I knew what was to be. The True Queen was coming, sooner than anyone anticipated.

Creek Summers

by Maura Pensinger

The day ends slowly, sun melting
like the ice cream we slurp out of sugar cones
into a thick July night
where fireflies flit their sporadic dance,
a frenzy of shifting constellations.
The forest grows thick behind us;
ivy, bramble, spindly tree limbs are prison gates
we never dare to cross
for fear of being eaten alive by thorns
as old oaks stand by, watching,
in their leathery skin.
Grass tickles our bare ankles; its claws are not
sharp so much as delicate
and the creek seems amused, taking a moment out of its rush
to play with the stones.

The Woman Behind The Glass

by Honora Quinn

Most days, when I'm not at school or hiding from Estelle in her labyrinthine closets, I lie on the couch and watch TV. More specifically I watch *Her*, my Mother, Lina Cave. She was an actress. Not one that you'd ordinarily know by name considering her short list of credits but I'm quite positive that if you saw her face on screen, you'd look at that woman behind the glass and go "oh! *Her*, yeah, she looks familiar,", if the pieces didn't click perfectly into place on the spot. She had two notable roles in her life, you might recall one over the other depending on your generation, but I'll overview them both. First there was *The Rowans*, from when she was a kid in the 80s and 90s. She played Ally Rowan, part of an ensemble mystery drama show. The other was *Weston: Medical* from the early 2000s. It was a science fiction vehicle, and she played a science officer by the name of Faye Valera. The latter was full of cheesy effects and form fitting costumes, the kind of thing that often still appear at cons and featured on cosplay accounts. The former had its fair share of convoluted plots and a house that was just *too* perfect to possibly be real. In those hours when I attempted to find an escape—

often when Estelle went out shopping or to brunch—Ally and Faye kept me company. I waffle and jump between the warm and predictable heists foiled by Ally and her family, and the sharp sci-fi adventures of Faye in a far-flung future. While it may seem from an outsider perspective that I have nothing better to do than rot my brain, or that my attention span is so corroded that I can't even watch a single episode to completion, I hope to assure you that there is a method to the madness.

I'm attempting to bring her back.

Now, don't worry this isn't about to be a whole *Frankenstein* thing. I'm not about to dig up anyone's graves in the dead of night… not again anyway… they put up a wrought-iron gate after the last time. But moving on from that—I have a theory that whenever you engage with a work of art, for a split second that person flashes back to us on Earth. If you pause your tv, find the right page or find just the right spot in the chorus of a song—you can reach through and bring them back, that they shine through the fiction for just long enough to come home. That is why I flip between shows the way I do; I stop once I reach my potential flash point—the crack—and move onto the next installment leaving the moment perfectly primed to bring Mother home. I haven't had the chance to truly try it out yet because of all the variables, I don't want to try it out on my Mother in less than perfect condition and leave her half stuck in Estelle's flat screen—god could you imagine the sound? But if I can only do this operation once I don't want to be stuck with

Shakespeare or Bach roaming around my house either. I can only imagine how they would disturb Estelle's perfect aesthetic home, it took a lot of hard work tearing it from the pages of magazines and niche corners of the internet. I needed a time when I knew it would work, an undeniable presence where no other outcome could be possible. I chose the book launch. *Estelle's* book launch. The forced nostalgia from the branding alone could bring anyone through the grime of space, time, and mortality.

"I first met Lina at an audition, we were scene partners for some horrible old drama—I doubt even most of us 'oldsters' in the room would have heard of it—it was a school scene, I asked Lina—I think her character was Marissa—if she would go with me to a dance. She said in reply that she'd have to sneak out but if I helped her, she would be the prettiest girl in the room, and everyone would love me. They were just lines, but she was right —not about the 'everyone loving me' thing I know the jury on that is still out for a lot of you with everything that has happened —but she *was* the prettiest, the kindest, and I miss her every day. Luckily for me and for history we would be quickly reunited on the set of…"

I began to zone out around the same time that Estelle's voice began to crack while she waxed on and on and on again about the impact my mother had on her—like I didn't hear enough of that from her every other day of the week. I had positioned myself in a far back corner of the bookstore as far from Estelle and her tears as I could get all while avoiding additional attention to my person. She was reading from her memoir, a mostly ghost-written book called *I Love Lina Cave And Other Mixed-Up Stories from Growing Up In Hollywood*, my mother was a very valuable part of the promotion process. The pinnacle of the promotion was tonight, the big launch and reading where I—Lina Cave's one and only child—was to make a personal appearance. I rarely appeared in public. Outside of grainy iPhone footage of me at school or the mall, there was shockingly limited evidence of my existence. It's not that I was never invited, Estelle always threw a shiny little invite my way, but my ongoing experiments were always just a better use of my time. But tonight, I was ready to grin and bear it, to endorse the book at the big launch and act like we were all on the same team.

So here I was. Sitting. Little did she, or anyone else, know that Lina herself would make an appearance and delightfully change the course of the evening! In my hours of watching, I was able to pinpoint the exact episodes where Lina peaked through the visages of Ally or Faye the most. In *The Rowans* Season 3 Episode 19 "…Do As The Rowan Do" a large part of the plot revolves around a prank war between the titular family and their occasional allies/foes/love objects, the St Bridgettes. Ally is forced into a confrontation with her best friend Celeste St. Bridgette which ends up being a trap. The girls get dumped in a blue goo which in turn becomes a clue and allows them to solve the mystery of the week but if you pause right after the goo is deployed, Ally and Celeste crack and for a moment all you see is Lina attempting to not laugh in a moment when she is scripted to be angry. For a moment my mother is back with us.

Upstairs, in just under an hour there would be a reception, filled to the ceiling with televisions showing every clip obtainable of my Mother, I made sure that my required episodes would be front and center—that everyone would see the spectacle. Now you may be wondering, 'how old will she be if I pull her from an episode when she is a teenager'. To be honest, I don't know. I hope that there will be a bit of a rubber band effect, that the body will bounce forward in time into the proper form for the year, but we will just have to wait and see, won't we?

While picking at my nailbeds, I noticed a lull in the theatrics. I had been so in my head, plotting with you, that I had forgotten what was expected from me tonight. Estelle was looking at me expectantly, a dainty arm extended. I stood, folding chair screeching against the floor before toppling with a loud crash. She didn't wince. Rather, it was more of an empathic stare—a pitiful stare—in fact everyone in the audience had turned to look at me. Faces glazed with an odd mix of genuine curiosity and a gleeful hate. The emotion just barely perceptible, hidden behind their false lashes and puffy lips. I raised my glass of cider; a toast would surely fit the situation. If I could well up some tears, I might be able to get out of this all together. Yet they all kept staring, blinking, and waiting.

Seeing no other way out of this, I began my trek to Estelle at her pulpit. The bookstore was packed, almost every seat filled with even more patrons standing on the perimeter. There was a frantic energy, like Estelle was some kind of god come to Earth rather than a has-been actress. Some of the faces I recognized, no one else from the show—*Weston: Medical*—was in attendance of course. They had all gone on to fruitful careers and didn't have to mine the dead for memories. But I locked eyes with an agent here, or a script writer there, the costume designer who had created the seemingly gravity defying suits that helped make my mother famous. Most of these familiar faces came without matching names. It elicited the same reaction I'd figured as looking through a scrapbook to look down upon family members long forgotten, yet to understand that they matter, or why.

Before too long I found myself at the edge of the stage, feet away from Estelle. We were wearing matching dresses, I realized. Under her too-hot-for-the-season mink, she was wrapped in the same lilac silk that I was. 'A Gift' the note had said. It had never occurred to me that it was yet another part of her marketing ploys, a show of solidarity. It would only confuse poor Mother when I pulled her out from behind the glass. However, that would be an issue for the future me to deal with, I grit my teeth, dug my fists into the slick fabric, and found my place at the older woman's side. There was a light smattering of applause at this, apparently at the mere fact that I was alive was revolutionary. Perhaps they were right, considering the odds on my matrilineal line. Estelle wrapped an arm around me, long red nails sinking into the floaty fabric.

"Lina's daughter Adelaide, her one and only heir, chose to join us tonight. And before we head upstairs for the refreshments, she's going to read a little something from my book,"

I looked at Estelle, with her hard protruding cheeks full of plastic, and glossy yet visibly chapped lips. She was putting me on the spot, I was never instructed to speak, just to smile and wave or at most throw in a nod of recognition here or there! I blinked. She poked me with another sharp nail, this time in the side.

"Come on, kid. It's the page with the pink flag." She looked out to the crowd with a 'kid's these days' shrug so I dragged my feet to the tune of tittering laughter. I found the pink flag and flipped the pages through my fingers. I could tell why she wanted me to read the preselected passage immediately. She wanted me, of all people, to read about my mother's death. My skin was buzzing, the silk sticking to my flesh like lava. I gripped the edges of the podium, running the tip of my index finger along the edge of the wood looking for a sharp point to exploit. I wanted to kill Estelle, an impulsive, jittery anger that I had worked hard to control in the past years. With her kindness there was always the fall, a task or deed she would always require of me. But my pinprick of pain—I found an adequate corner to push upon—would ground me. I knew from experience that making a scene with Estelle felt great in the moment, that she would never react with a crowd but the moment we were alone I would be made to pay for my mistreatment. She hoped that the audience would keep me in check too. I looked down at the title, perched on top of the page in heavy bold letters.

CHAPTER 15: DEATH IN AVALON

I paused after reading the title, mainly to give myself a moment to gear up to barrel through three straight pages, but the audience clearly needed it too. The air was still.

"'I still remember where I was when I heard the news that Lina was dead. It was October 4th, the year her *Weston: Med* follow-up show swept the Emmys. I was singing on a cruise line, top of the marquee and everything. There had been an accident on set; while carrying her daughter—'" I paused to clear my throat "'she slipped down the stairs from her trailer. Striking her head and succumbing to the impact. They had moved production to Avalon, Massachusetts for the summer and I still have the postcard she sent. Featuring a sunset, the cheesy 'wish you were here' the works. She had told me how excited she was to stick her feet in the Atlantic. She never got the chance.'"

Again, another inhale. The lava sensation had largely subsided, but it didn't help my unease. I could feel the eyes that traced every aspect of my being, from the flyaway hairs on my head to the irregular pat-a-pat-pat-a-pat of my shoe on the ground. The worst of it was over. Yet I still had to be the one to disclose Estelle's cruise escapades to the world for the first time, arguably worse that and gory details about my mother I could be forced to read aloud.

And then it was over.

And then it was *time.*

I threw an over cheery smile out to the crowd when I finished my reading and turned on a dime to embrace Estelle. The evening could only be hers for so much longer I might as well help make it count. She pinched my side lightly, affectionately and bent close to whisper in my ear.

"Good job. Let's bring this home huh?"

I didn't speak any further but matched her conspiratorial expression.

"Custom cocktails and other refreshments will be served upstairs, go on and make your way, make yourselves at home, Adelaide and I will join you shortly." She threw a kiss at the crowd, and they roared in applause. The masses began to dissipate, and Estelle linked her arm through mine, dragging me towards the back elevator.

"We must make a grand entrance," she smiled, brushing some smudged makeup from my cheeks.

"They loved you," I said, worried anything else would cause my scheme to burst from my lips.

"They love *Her*," she sighed, "any adoration for us is just a sidecar."

Since my mother's death Estelle had attempted to care for me, she paid for my education anything I could need. But within the first few months, it became clear that she was using me to replace her friendship with my mother, have another pretty little doll to spoil. I never wanted a replacement mother, even from those days I had my theory brewing and I used to worry that she'd see that Estelle replaced her and leave us both—again! I wasn't as smart then, but my stubbornness caused a rift between Estelle and myself, just large enough for the ghost of Lina Cave to float. It didn't matter anymore however, because tonight it wouldn't be a ghost, or a forcible memory but the real deal.

We arrived at the balcony to fanfare, but Estelle was quickly swept away into the crowd. I parked myself at a standing table in perfect view of the TV that I had personally programmed. They all ran on a loop rotating through episodes, clips, or even some apparent edits taken from social media, but this one only played my episode. It was early in the plot, the concept of the prank war just introduced, so I allowed myself a trip to the bar for a Shirley Temple—extra strong, hold the cherries. It couldn't have taken more than a couple minutes. I expected to arrive back at the table right as the B Plot would have been introduced… but I had missed it? I sipped on my collapsing paper straw as the final scene played out. The five Rowan children sat on a garbage bag covered couch as they were all coated in a rainbow of multicolored goo and particulate. I watched as the camera came in for a tight shot of my mother, she had made a joke although I couldn't recall what exactly, and the camera moved right as she crossed her arms and rolled her eyes. Fade to black, roll credits. I *had* missed it.

The night was still young, so it was no real bother. She would just make a later appearance than expected. Flights got delayed all the time! The second round I watched the screen diligently, watched the A and B plots entangle, watched Celeste and Ally agree to meet, and then the crab cakes came to my table… this time I looked away for less than a second, but I missed the crack. I took the entire platter of crab cakes and set it on my table preparing for my third viewing. My hands were all greasy anyway and Mother wouldn't like that. It would ruin her clothes! I was being considerate by finishing my food before greeting her!

The third viewing I practically had my nose on the glass. Only moving to take a draw of my Shirley or breath without fogging the glass. Soon we were back to Celeste and Ally. They entered the garage, the shadow of the buckets held above them visible. I breathed in deep, fingers grazing the surface. The goo fell, covering them both, Lina appeared, and I struck.

I had considered how pain would end up factoring in my experiment, but I hadn't expected exactly that it would happen to me. A sharp prang enveloped my fist. I bit back a smile; it must just be part of the process I reasoned. She was a woman behind the glass and there was no other way but *through*. I had another show, Lina was still on screen, so I struck again and this time—spiderwebs. The glass splintered along the face of the screen, this was an older model the kind with knobs and thick interior guts. I figured I would need the space to pull her out, smart huh?

I took a step back, waiting for something, anything, to happen. The crowds behind me had largely hushed, an energy in the air like they too couldn't wait to see. I waited a moment, and then another but there was nothing. Lina was still frozen on the surface, so I jumped to strike one last time. But arms encircled my torso, and I was yanked back away from the jagged glass and my one shot at victory.

It was Estelle, I smelled her perfume and the faint scent of alcohol before I ever saw her face. She brought us down to the ground, petting my hair with the back of her hand. The image eventually went dark, my mother returned to the land of the fictional and Ally Rowan would soon wash her hair and leave her gooey adventure behind. I had failed, perhaps. Made a fool of myself and my guardian, yes. But it had been a valiant effort, and Estelle was treating my endeavor—and my person—in this moment with something just short of love. After all the years of discourse, of her affectionate attempts gone awry, she was the only person I could picture being with me, the only person who deserved to watch Lina Cave walk out of that screen alongside me.

If she ever did.

When.

Soon the tears mixed with mascara and broken glass would be swept away and come morning the gravity of my situation would reach the outer world. The almost rhyming pair of *denial* and *wild* would find their ways onto the gossip pages, but for now all there was, was Estelle, myself, and that woman trapped behind the glass.

Forevermore

by Brendan Sack

The sky gleamed a rosy red with clouds coming from the west. A ravening coyote traveled along the royal forest front carrying a bow on his right shoulder and a quiver on his left. Dirt blemished the coyote's purple tunic. The coyote traveled with his servants for a morning hunt, but after the coyote chased a large, charming rabbit down a river, he became separated.

The coyote's eyes pinpointed a black and white speck of hair from a distance and out came the coyote's old friend, the badger, from the royal forest front. It is not odd that the coyote and badger would meet while hunting for each owned land near one another, but the badger appeared alone like the coyote. The badger approached the coyote revealing his purple tunic similar to the coyote and equally blemished with dirt. A sharp sword dangled on the badger's belt in its scabbard.

"Good morning," said the badger.

"Good morning," responded the coyote. "Where might be your servants?"

The badger's face became smug. "A large and fair rabbit hopped near me by the forest front, so I burrowed into the forest in pursuit, but it seems my servants were not skilled enough to keep up."

"It seems we have been after the same critter," said the coyote. "And I have lost my servants too."

"If we follow along the royal forest front, we'll reach our lands, but I do desire that rabbit," said the badger.

"Why?" asked the coyote. "Have there been food issues?"

"No, food is not of concern," answered the badger. "You must know it would be worthwhile to place that beautiful rabbit beside my riches for an exotic display."

The coyote smirked with a cunning desire. "Let me accompany you, and I can help you catch that critter."

"If you offer assistance, then I cannot refuse," said the badger.

The sky continued to gleam a rosy red as the coyote and badger traveled into the royal forest to search. It would not be a long search, however, as the badger had last seen the large rabbit hopping east toward where there is a cliffside. Soon, in the coyote and badger's sight appeared the exotic critter. The rabbit's fur shone brightly like a pearl, and his size could feed an entire village for good. The pearly rabbit hopped into a bush ahead, and the badger began to draw his sword from his scabbard.

"What are you doing?" asked the coyote.

"I am going to burrow into that bush with my sword," answered the badger. "You do not hunt rabbits with a sword," said the coyote.

The badger's face became maddened. "You do not hunt rabbits with those arrows of yours either. Just look how big the arrowheads are."

Before the coyote could respond, the rabbit hopped out of the bush he was in and traveled away from the coyote and badger. The coyote and badger chased after the critter for a few minutes, passing through bushes and dodging trees until the critter hopped in a tall shrubbery set. Both the coyote and badger took a breath before advancing into the tall shrubbery set whereupon the other side arose a sight to behold. Two tombs stood only feet from the coyote and badger in an open field. It occurred then that the tombs began to open.

The left tomb opened to only a coat inside, but the coyote became startled by the sight. The coat was a fur coat, and its fur belonged to a coyote. In a flash, the coat began to move, and feet belonging to a coyote climbed out of the tomb. The coat wrapped itself to sit on the ground and revealed a coyote's head. A paw emerged from the coat holding an arrow.

"What are my eyes seeing?" wailed the coyote.

The right tomb began to open more, which caught the badger's attention. Inside the tomb sat a hat, but this hat made the badger vomit. Badger fur assembled the hat. Like the coat, the hat began to climb from the tomb where a badger's head and paws became visible. The hat flopped onto the ground, and its paw carried an arrow the same as the coat.

"I am going to flee!" bawled the badger.

The badger's head from the hat turned toward the badger and said, "Do not flee, for we are not demons."

"Who are you?" asked the coyote.

The coyote's head from the coat looked upon the coyote. "We are your forefathers who you disrespect, so listen."

"When we were upon the Earth, we took pride in our riches," said the badger hat. "For that, we now suffer," said the coyote coat.

"So be mindful of us," said the badger hat.

The rosy sky above appeared darker, and the coyote remembered the clouds coming from the west. Rain began to fall from the sky, and thunder erupted in the distance. Everything remained still except for the thunderstorm. Neither the coyote, the badger, the coat, or the hat moved for seventeen minutes. As the area became darker, the coat and hat disappeared, and the tombs vanished. All the clouds vanished from above, and the sky returned to the rosy red of morning.

The coyote and badger headed home from their hunt without a murmur. When they arrived, they sold their riches for a trap. Then, the coyote and badger placed the trap by the royal forest front and waited. One day, the large pearly rabbit was caught by the trap, whereupon the coyote and badger cared for the critter forevermore.

Question

by Karly Gerow

Why does the moon never talk back?
I sit and wait in my suffocating silence
praying for some kind of response.
The crickets begin chirping in its absence
and the fireflies dance in the wheat.
The path I took to be closer to you brought me up to
stones and stars,
creating an endless lavender haze.
Even as it rained down with acid and fire, I held on.
Just dying to hear some part of your melodic voice,
angelic to my ears: instead, the crow shrieks
A blood-curdling cry,
feathers falling from the sky.
My bones stiff and muscles sore
only one set of footprints waiting for me at the bottom of this
hill I would soon die on.
All of this time wasted on wishful thinking
searching for an answer I thought you would give me.
So I'll ask again but this time I think I know the answer.
Why does the moon never talk back?
Because I was the only one listening.

Too Late

by Karly Gerow

It was already too late. Aisle four of the rest stop in New Hope, a small town founded by the great people of the North, forever changed in one moment. There stood a mother and her son on a rainy afternoon. She, lost in concentration, the boy in ignorant bliss. The woman stared off at the countless pickle jars and cursed under her breath at the absurdity of this task. She moved into the Kosher Dill section, black drab garments trailing her lean body. Her son, Jake, an odd fellow but a loving soul to all he meets, watched in bewilderment at this new place. Sure, he'd seen colors and foods and jars before but none like these. No, these held a special place in his heart.

The strange objects inside floated in some kind of goo, stickers with characters he could not read, the reflective glass he was transfixed on. But of course, they also possessed this pesky thing. Covers with yellow and green, puncture marks to secure, and the ultimate "come open me" invitation for Jake. Stuck in the sticky cart with his tight black shirt and pants his mother placed him in, Jack squirmed to maneuver himself closer to the shelf. His stubby fingers 1, 2, 3, 4, and 5 on each hand flexed and wiggled as they drew near.

The pads of his hands brushed the container, which sent a spark of excitement to his brain. Jack moved in, and got a grip on the jar, pulling it back. Slowly he traveled over the rift between shelf and cart, his eyes dazzled in accomplishment. Just as he was about to receive his prize, a nice large whatever-the-heck those were, Jack's mother stood up and stared right at him.

Then, almost like a slow-motion video, Jack's hands released the pickles to hide his face. Fear and adrenaline pumped through his brain. The church bell rang three times in the distance. A last call of sorts to those who wished to say goodbye to an old woman. She wore pearls dangled from her ears and hung around her neck. A faint remnant of a smile hidden behind the attempts to return color to her face. There stood her family, all but two, at her casket wishing her the very best in the afterlife.

Escapade of a Quasi-Hero

by Brendan Sack

The school day finally ended, and the hero hastened into the halls. An adventure awaited him, but first, he must obtain his sword. The hero knew exactly where to find one.

"Let me borrow your sword squire," the hero said.

Like the sword in the stone, the hero grabbed a sword from a baseball player's backpack and held it high. It was a righteous sword made to deliver a home run. Only the most skilled could handle it.

The hero ventured outside, but an ill feeling came upon him. Shouts erupted from behind. Unknown figures were giving chase from yonder. Quickly, the hero ran and hopped onto a steed, but the steed would not gallop.

"What is wrong?" asked the hero.

The hero realized the steed had broken legs and looked sick from its bluish appearance. Unable to escape, the hero jumped from the steed and drew his sword for whatever approached. Nine bandits materialized from all angles.

"Advance and feel pain by my sword," announced the hero.

"Give me back my bat," said one bandit.

"You are after my sword? You are a fool if you expect to steal it," the hero said.

The hero raised his sword higher, prepared if a skirmish would occur, but nine against one seemed considerably unfair. No matter, however, the hero remembered his training to parry attacks.

The skirmish was fierce, and many recorded the encounter. In the end, ten boys stayed home from school the next couple of weeks.

As You Are in Your Bedroom in 2024, 2:56am

by Lara Chamoun

Pixels breathe
and you're stitched to your avatar
And you cut yourself because of who you were pretending to
be.

You are what you are,
what you pose,
what ricochets back at you
from your rectangular, glowing box of everything.

You show all your friends
that you want to be an emoji
and they materialize there on the screens,
right there.

Their icons are the shape
of bruises and vintage vape burns.
Cigarettes are the bartered currency of wounds,
smoke biting the noose-snakes around your neck
as you choke.

There's a tutorial for everything and
they all open with the same sound.

There you are in your dark messy bedroom
and in the light of the screen
you could be everything you've ever wanted to be,
except you've never wanted anything.

You have it all;
you eat your world whole
when you open your curtains
because this brightness is so acute
that it burns.

Your friends tell you
to smash your fist through the window
until the world goes dark.
You see in the glass that
you are not what you are.

Alive to Speak It

by Lara Chamoun

Houses creak
when you've been quiet for too long
and the pipes have forgotten how to hum.
The walls tap against themselves in waiting and
the air goes sharp with hunger.

You've tried making ripples with your voice
by whispering your name into mirrors
and letting them shatter your tongue
like light breaking through glasses of water.

You wonder what sound was
before you went missing
and you lost your mind like a crown,
tilting and slipping and gone.
There was a sound for falling once—
you can't remember the burden of gold.

You wear it like you've learned it
and it grows up your throat until
you cough up heavy shards
of blood-iron
and you're missing the absence of a weight.

It splits you open
a second skin.
Out come the uncut stones:
you are everything they say you are.
You balance that carefully: screaming
is a pebble on your tongue.
The parting of your lips is
the slow, reluctant tearing
of a body that's forgotten how to be
alive enough to speak.

Sound itself is reluctant
to return to an anatomy of rage.
It scratches at your ribs and waits because
it knows your voice will crack.

So, so quiet and suspicious,
you are everything they say you're not.

Being Used is Like Being a Trash Can

by Karly Gerow

Being used is like being a trash can.
I am like a trash can;
composed of many colors, structures, designs
wild to the imagination, all different.

I am made of stainless steel
unable to rust and reliable.
My chemical compounds made less toxic to protect others.
Wind and rain won't shake me so I'm vital
during your torrential storms.

Though you have a lid, and I do not,
my walls are sturdy
I could hold twenty times my weight
while you have a barrier.
Consuming everything you no longer want,
a quick eject sequence, storing your waste
until someone can't bear the stench any longer.

Swapped out with new liners
to project my gentle shape,
but you forget the hole in the bag.

No, I'd never complain
when last night's hot home-cooked dinner
or your old blue nail polish
or the Coca-Cola from school
ruined my protective coating.

Keeping safe your undesirables until I too, become unwanted
thrown out with the rest of the garbage.

Scare Town

by Kiki Hawkins

"C'mon, Josie. It doesn't have to be perfect," I said as I watched my friend re-draw a star near the corner of her eye for the fifth time. I tried to snag the eyeliner she was drawing with, but she yanked her hand away. The butterflies in my stomach were flapping so hard I thought I was going to puke with excitement. I didn't want to be late.

"Stooop," She whined, "You're gonna make me mess up. It *needs* to be perfect."

"Why?"

"Because I want it to."

I couldn't argue with that. I had to admit, it did really pull the look together. I just think she could've been done the first time. I checked the time on my phone. Over five minutes wasted on this, and the clock was ticking.

She wore a moss green tank top, despite it being the end of October. Her eyeshadow matched her top near perfect. It complimented her dark brown hair and eyes really nicely; the color scheme reminded me of the forest.

She finally decided her star was good enough, so she moved on to picking jewelry. Her necklaces jangled as she sifted through her jewelry box. She held one in her hand, examined it for a moment, then tossed it to me. I caught it with my face.

"*Ow*," I complained.

"Sorry," she, very unapologetically, apologized.

Having done this thousands of times before, I knew she wanted me to wear it. I'm not big on jewelry, but she adores it. I'm like a blank canvas for her, open to any earrings, bracelets, necklaces, and rings. She always managed to pick out just the right things.

I looked in her mirror while I slipped on the simple black chain onto my neck. It stuck out against my pale skin. It still worked somehow. Maybe because it matched my black hair.

Josie appeared next to me and started layering some necklaces she picked out for herself. Looking at the two of us next to each other, I was reminded of how we looked like polar opposites in some aspects. I had shoulder length, wavy black hair while she had waist length brown straight hair. I was as pale as a ghost, and she had gorgeous brown skin. I had eyes that looked like the sky on a sunny day and hers looked like chocolate fudge.

After fiddling with her necklaces and earrings for a bit, she leaned back to admire the two of us in the mirror.

"God, we are *gorgeous*. Fabulous. Amazing. Spectacular." She did a new pose for each adjective she listed. I laughed.

"Also, Sarah, your outfit," she made a chef's kiss gesture, "even I wouldn't have thought of pairing those pieces together."

She was referencing my open brown flannel with a low-cut blue top underneath. I hadn't thought about it either. I threw on the first thing I saw over my shirt so my mom wouldn't freak out and tell me I was "going to catch hypothermia and freeze to death".

"Thanks." I smiled at her. She loves to give out compliments like candy on Halloween, and I always enjoyed receiving them.

I heard a buzz, and Josie pulled her phone out of her jean pocket.

"Eden's waiting for us," she told me. Eden and two of our other friends, Alice and Connor, were coming with us to this new haunted house called Scare Town. From overhearing some classmates' conversations, I gathered that it's a decently scary place. I couldn't wait to be scared absolutely shitless. My friends call me an adrenaline junkie because I love doing stuff like this, watching horror movies, and occasionally shoplifting. (For legal reasons, that last one was totally a joke)

Anyways, Josie and I left her room, said bye to her mom, and joined our friends in the car.

Before I could even finish scooting into the middle seat in the back row next to Connor, Eden turned around to look at me and said, "Dude, do you know how long you take to walk out of the damn house?" There was no bite to her words, she just likes to be dramatic for shits and giggles.

Josie responded for me. "Girl, you texted us less than 60 seconds ago."

Eden rolled her eyes and mumbled in a mocking way, but I could see the ends of her lips curling up before she turned away.

I chuckled and buckled my seatbelt.

Eden started up the car and pulled out of the driveway. The radio turned on with the rest of the car, blaring Epic the Musical. I guessed from that that either Conner or Alice was on aux. The both had a shared obsession over the musical.

"Really? Epic? It's Halloween. Shouldn't we play Ghostbusters or Thriller or something?" I teased.

"Absolutely not. The Vengeance Saga *just* came out." Connor responded. "Like, quite literally today."

"Besides," Alice added, "this saga is the best thing ever. Even Eden likes it."

Eden clicked on the headlights since it was getting dark. "A, I only like the last song. B, you say each saga is the best thing ever."

Josie interrupted with a loud groan. "Yeah, okay, enough with your nerd rambles. I want to hear about Scare Town."

"I heard someone died there." Eden turned off the music.

"Really?"

Connor snorted. "That did *not* happen. We live in a small town; everyone would be talking about it."

I feel like that would be a perfect scenario for a Scream movie. Kids go to a haunted house, think the killer is a scare actor, but get killed instead.

"That happened in a book I read." I added. "There was this killer guy pretending to be a scare actor. Stabbed this one guy right through the throat."

"Eww." Alice whined. She wasn't a fan of gore in the same way I was. Or scary things. I'm actually still surprised she came with us. "Unless you want to clean up my regurgitated dinner from this car, please stop talking."

I laughed but decided to be quiet now since cleaning up vomit isn't exactly my favorite thing to do.

Conversation slowed down a bit and I stared out the window at the dark scenery around us. Well, I couldn't figure out which window to stare out of since I was in the middle seat, so it was more like switching between my options.

Eventually, the GPS took us down this dirt road with a big glowing Scare Town sign. I could hear gravel crunching under the wheels of the car as Eden found us a parking spot.

Once we were all out of the car, I could see everyone easier now. The parking lot was tiny and rimmed with yard lanterns sticking up from the ground on stakes.

Eden was dressed in all black. Black jeans, black tank top (what is up with my friends and wearing tank tops in October?), black eyeliner, black choker, even black hair. She also had mushroom earrings that she probably made herself. It brought a small bit of color to her outfit along with her green eyes.

It was a bit of an odd combo, whimsical earrings with a monotone outfit, but she made it work.

I looked over at Connor. He had a flannel like me, but his was red. He wore a green tee underneath. He had on the same ripped jeans he wore every single day. His silver chain necklace matched his circular glasses. His hair looked like he finally gave it its monthly wash. It was all brown and fluffy.

Josie, Connor, and Eden walked ahead with Alice and I behind them.

Alice fiddled with the ends of her blue sweater, her favorite piece of clothing she owns. She's always been quite a bit more anxious than the rest of us, and with the way her eyes darted around a little more than usual, I figured she needed a little more reassurance that nothing bad is going to happen.

"Alice?" I asked quietly, not wanting to pull the attention of our other friends.

She dropped her hands, probably trying to hide her fidgeting. "Hm?"

"You good?"

"Yeah. Yeah, I'm fine." She stared off to the side at the big empty field behind the parking lot. "Eden's story freaked me out a bit, though. Just… What if something *does* happen?"

I shook my head. "Nothing's gonna happen. It's perfectly safe. Besides, that's your lucky sweater right? If anyone dies, it's not going to be you."

She turned back to me. "That's not helpful."

"Sorry."

"Sorry, that was rude of me."

I waved my hand in an *it's fine* gesture. I didn't really know how else to comfort her. I wanted to make her feel better though. Maybe I could give her a compliment?

"Uh, I like your bow." I pointed at the little pink ribbon in her blonde hair. It pulled together her whole pastel aesthetic. Her sweater was blue, like I mentioned, but it had big square patches of different shades. The soft pink of her bow went with it nicely.

"Thank you," she mumbled.

I figured she just didn't want to talk anymore, so I turned my attention to the entrance of Scare Town. Eden was giving our tickets to the check-in-ticket-collector guy. He opened the gate, and we walked into the monstrosity of a wait line.

***

I sauntered out of the haunted house with my friends in tow, giggling like a mad man. My stomach hurt from laughing so hard the past hour. Alice was clinging to Connor's arm like it was the only thing not trying to murder her. He looked very unbothered, but I could see his hands shaking. Josie looked like she'd just had the adrenaline high of her life. Eden seemed to be glad it was over, but she was still smiling.

Out back, they had a concession stand and a couple of wooden picnic tables. String lights illuminated the area. Other than that, it was near pitch black.

All of us got snacks and sat at a table.

"Okay," Connor pointed his hot dog at the rest of us, "scariest parts. Go."

Eden blurted out, "That fuckass clown, dude. The one with the big knife in the area with all those strobe lights."

I groaned. "That guy was *freaky*, oh my God." I took a sip of my Dr. Pepper. "I think the worst though was that black plague doctor. I nearly shat my pants when he started chasing us."

"You screamed so loud!" Josie laughed.

"You were worse than me!" I argued.

Alice intervened and wagged a french fry at us. "You *both* screamed like little girls." She teased before eating one of her fries.

"What was scariest for you?" Conner asked Alice with a mouthful of hot dog. I made a mental note to teach him manners later.

"All of it! It was terrible!" she cried.

I grinned at her. "But we all survived, didn't we?" She kicked me under the table.

I glanced over at Josie, who was sitting right next to her. I was going to ask her what the worst part for her was, but she was staring off into the distance. I tried to see what she was looking at, but through the blackness of the night all I could see was just corn fields. It goes up on a hill and then you can't see anything past. No trees or anything. "What're you lookin' at?"

"I wonder what's out there." She cocked her head to the side.

Connor reached over and stole one of the fries that came with Josie's burger. "Wanna find out?"

"Yes!" Eden said.

"No!" Alice said.

I stared out at the field. Now that it was brought up, I was kind of curious what could hide in there. I shrugged. "I'm down."

"That's the spirit." Conner grinned.

"Are you *crazy*?" Alice said. "I know you guys are—excuse my language—batshit crazy, but this is a bit much, don't you think?"

Eden slurped the last of her lemonade. "You don't have to come with."

Alice huffed and crossed her arms, checking out of the conversation.

"Nah, we've got to get her out of her shell." Conner licked ketchup from his fingers. "She never does anything fun with us!"

"She *does not* have to go." Having been at the end of Eden's death stare before, I'm not shocked at how fast Conner backed down.

He stood up and started grabbing trash off the table. "Whatever. I'm throwing the trash away and then *I'm* going." His flannel fluttered in the breeze as he walked away.

Alice had her hands clasped tightly together in her lap and was staring down at the table. The smallest bit of arguing always got her like this. It was kind of annoying, but I never said anything. I didn't need to make her feel worse.

Eden patted her shoulder. She was never very good at comforting. She did always make an effort to defend Alice, though. They had a strange kind of bond. It was cute.

Conner returned and stood at the end of the picnic table with his hands on his hips. "Alright. Who's coming with?"

All of us stood up, including Alice.

Eden looked at her. "Alice, you don—"

"I'm coming," She grumbled.

Eden sighed but didn't say anything more.

We made the short walk to the edge of the cornfield. The stalks looked grey in the darkness. Away from the lights of the concession stand, it was a lot harder to see my friends. The corn wasn't lined up at all, which was odd, but it would make it harder for us to get caught, which is a plus.

"Wait." Josie held her hand out. "How are we going to find our way out?"

"Well, the corn will probably be messed up a bit by us walking through it right? We'll follow our path back. If not, we'll find a way out if we walk long enough," I said.

"How comforting. How are we going to see?"

Conner pulled his phone out and turned on the flashlight. He shot Josie a grin.

She shrugged. "Okay. You go first." She pushed him forward through the first stalks.

"Hey!" Conner laughed as he stumbled forward.

Josie laughed and waved her hand in a shooing motion. He rolled his eyes and kept walking, the corn shuffling against each other as he made a path through.

Josie followed, then Eden and Alice side by side, then me in caboose.

I hesitated for just a second. The small hairs on the back of my neck stood up. Something was wrong. My head told me I'm paranoid, but my gut told me to turn back immediately. I shook my head and pushed through the corn to catch up to my friends.

After maybe fifteen minutes, we'd made it an adequate distance into the field. I looked behind me and saw the corn had in fact not stayed bent. My hands started to shake. What if we couldn't actually find a way out? I couldn't even see the haunted house due to the corn being taller than me.

"Hey, um, guys?" I started. "We—"

Conner turned around and held his hand out. "Shut up."

"What?" What was his problem?

He put his finger to his lips and cocked his head. "I said shut up. Do you hear that?"

All of us stopped moving and tried to hear what he was talking about. It was an eerie silence. I glanced around, my gaze shooting from corn stalk to corn stalk. I heard nothing but corn rustling in the wind.

Eden sighed. "Dude, what are you going on about? There's nothing."

"Wait." Conner insisted.

"Conn—"

"*Wait.*"

A dark figure popped out, and we all screamed. My heart jumped to my throat. Alice stumbled back and fell down. I reached down and quickly helped her up before taking a step back myself. She brushed dirt off the back of her jeans.

Conner's phone light shined on the figure. They wore a Ghostface sort of cloak, but their mask was a simple white circle with an emoji-like smile printed on it. What the hell is a scare actor doing all the way out here?

Eden must've had the same thought because she said, "God! You scared the shit out of us! What are you *doing* out here?"

The person simply cocked their head and took a step closer to her. Something shiny glinted in their hand under Conner's phone light. I barely had time to realize what it was before it was embedded in Eden's chest.

It felt like everything slowed down. Eden didn't even scream. Her deep, shaky gasp was almost worse. I felt sick.

The knife is yanked back out by Mr. Stabber Guy. Eden fell down and clutched at her bloodied chest.

Conner immediately sprang forward and tackled the guy. "Go! Run!" He told us.

I may be a total dick for this, but I did not need to be told twice. I yanked Eden up and bolted. Josie followed behind us.

I ran and ran. The cornstalks hit me over and over again, scratching at my skin, but I kept running. I needed to get away. My heart pounded like crazy. Blood rushed in my ears. I glanced behind me to check on my friends. Eden was seriously lagging behind. We all slowed to a stop.

Eden was panting hard. "Can we just… sit down?"

"Yeah." Josie's voice shook. "Yeah, we can sit."

Eden stumbled trying to get on the ground. She kind of fell more than she sat.

Josie and I kneeled. I crawled forward to Eden and shone my phone light over her chest. Her black tank top just looked wet, but knowing what it was wet *from* made me nearly throw up. I closed my eyes and took a breath before looking again.

"How bad is it?" Eden asked me. Her breath was ragged even though we were sitting now.

I gently moved her top to get a better look at the wound. There was so much red. My eyes stung with tears begging to be released. The knife was really close to her heart. Not in any situation would she survive.

"It's—it's okay." My breaking voice was probably giving me away. "It's not that bad."

"Sarah," Eden said. Looking at her sickly pale face made my heart clench. "Just tell me the truth."

My lip quivered. I shook my head. Eden's face softened. She didn't look scared at all. How? She knew she was going to die and she wasn't scared?

Josie moved over and helped Eden lay down. She hadn't said anything yet. I don't know if she could. She grabbed Eden's hand tightly. I put my phone back in my pocket and held onto the other hand.

Neither of us knew what to say. What are you even supposed to say? We all sat in silence. Cold tears streamed down my cheeks. I held Eden's hand until it went limp.

I broke out into total ugly sobbing. Josie's arms wrapped around me. Her face buried in my shoulder. Eden was *dead*. I was furious at Conner for suggesting we go out here. I was angry at Josie for being the reason Conner got the idea. It was irrational, I know, but I couldn't help the rage from boiling up.

Corn shuffled behind us. Far away, but still too close for comfort. I whipped my head around and tried to stifle my involuntary gasps for air.

"We have to go," I whispered.

Josie's hand gripped my shoulder to keep me from moving. "It could be Alice and Conner."

"Well, we don't know! Do you want to die like Eden?" I whispered louder.

"Shush. Listen," she told me and paused for a few seconds. "That sounds like two people running. Our friends."

I rolled my eyes. "Or it's Knife Guy chasing Alice because he already killed Conner."

"We don't know that."

"We don't know anything!" I shouted.

Josie opened her mouth to speak but was cut off by two people bursting through the stalks. I covered my mouth to keep from screaming. I relaxed once I recognized my friends standing in front of me. Conner had a long cut across his cheek and new rips in his jeans. Alice had dirt smeared across her sweater.

Alice stared down at Eden's body with wide eyes and a pale face. "Oh my God. Eden…" she whispered.

"Look," Conner said, "we don't have much time. He's right behind us. Run now, mourn later."

Josie and I scrambled up. I could hear footsteps getting closer.

"How close is he?" Josie asked, fidgeting with her necklace.

"I don't know, but we should—" He made a gurgling noise as the point of a dagger made its way through his neck.

Alice screamed and scrambled over next to Josie. Conner dropped to his knees then fell all the way forward. Standing behind Conner was the sick fuck with the smiling mask.

The three of us quickly regained our senses and darted away as fast as we could. The guy didn't immediately start chasing us, but soon enough we could hear him running after us.

"How do we get out of here?" Alice heaved.

"I don't know. Just keep running. We have to get out eventually." Josie answered.

My lungs burned and my legs were ready to buckle. If the dude ended up killing me, at least I wouldn't have to run anymore. With all the trauma this is going to leave, would it be for the better? Assuming Alice and Josie survive, they might need me though. Whatever. What happens is out of my control anyways.

We made it to the small hill I had seen earlier, meaning we were pretty far out. It also meant that there could be an escape on the other side.

I was seriously not excited to run up a hill while actively fighting the urge to collapse, but I did it anyway.

The cornstalks stopped directly on top of the hill. We had reached the end, and I could see sweet, sweet salvation. At the bottom of the hill was a farm. And a tractor. A way to get away from the man with the knife.

My friends and I shared a quick look of ecstaticness before rushing down the hill. We didn't dare look back as we bolted for the farm tractor. I was pretty sure none of us knew how to drive one, but it's life or death. We had to figure it out.

We reached the machine and got a better look. It had one driver's seat and a cart in the back. Alice appointed herself as the driver.

"The key is already in here. Get in the back," she said.

"Wait, why the hell would the key be in there? It's a trap." Josie decided.

Alice turned her head around to look at her. "It's a small town. People don't expect things to get stolen. Now do what I told you and get in the back!"

Hearing her yell was a bit jarring. She's never raised her voice. I would've questioned how she knew how to drive a tractor, but that seemed like an issue for later.

Josie and I hopped in the cart and sat down. I looked back to the hill to scan for Knife Guy. He was at the bottom of the hill. My heart beat so hard I thought it would break my ribs.

"Alice, we need to go now." I ushered.

She was fiddling with levers and buttons. "I know that!"

Finally, I could feel the engine rumbling under me. I breathed a deep sigh of relief as the ground started moving under us. I tried to give Josie a smile, but she was scanning over the cart floor intently.

"What're you looking for?" I asked.

"My earring. It fell."

"That's what you're worried about right now?"

Josie rolled her eyes. "Yes." She glanced up at me for a second and then did a double take with wide eyes. "Sarah, behind you!"

I whipped my head around to see the knife guy about ten feet from the tractor and his knife hurdling right towards my face. My heart stopped and I tried to move out of the way. I felt the cold metal send searing pain through my neck. The knife clattered against the wood of the cart.

I fully forgot how to breathe for a moment. My trembling hands instinctively shot up to clutch my wound, a deep slit across my throat. My skin against my open flesh made another spike shoot through me. I gasped.

Josie was instantly holding me. "Oh my God… Oh my God, Sarah."

"What?!" Alice cried from the driver's seat. "What's 'oh my God'?!"

I wanted to say something, *anything*, but all I could force out was groan.

Josie gripped my hand. "No, it's okay. We can fix this." I wasn't sure if she was telling me that or herself.

I shook my head and gave her a weak smile. I knew I wouldn't survive. The edge of my vision was already fuzzing with black. Josie's words were far away. I now understood why Eden didn't seem scared to die.

Tears dripped down Josie's cheek. She seemed to understand what I was thinking. Her hands pressed mine against her chest.

I couldn't even feel it. The parts of me I could still feel felt like heavy ice cubes.

Alice was saying stuff, but she was just background noise to me.

Darkness was closing in faster. I was okay with dying, but I felt a pang of guilt for Josie and Alice. How could I leave them at a time like this? I also knew it wasn't my fault, and for once in my whole life, that satisfied me.

I spent my very last fragment of energy to mouth, *I love you.* Josie sobbed.

Darkness filled my vision, and my very last thought was "I hope she'll be okay."

The Unrighteous Raccoon

by Brendan Sack

The raccoon found the squirrel in the woods and hugged him with open arms. It had been a while since he could greet anyone at dusk, and he was friends with the squirrel. However, a desire came to steal from the squirrel, so the raccoon stole cherries from the squirrel.

"Why have you taken my cherries?" the squirrel asked.

The raccoon hesitated. He looked at the cherries he stole and felt a piercing guilt that tore into his mind. It is a raccoon's job to steal, but doing so was wrong and would hurt his friend.

However, he would not be a raccoon if he did not steal. The raccoon contemplated his guilt and decided to return the cherries.

"I apologize for stealing. I cannot make any excuse for myself, so please forgive me," the raccoon pleaded.

"I accept your apology, but do not steal again," said the squirrel as he scuttled away towards his home.

At dawn, the raccoon met the squirrel again. They greeted each other, but a desire came upon the raccoon to steal, and he once again took cherries from the squirrel.

"Why have you stolen from me again?" the squirrel asked.

A bad feeling struck the raccoon's head and left him feeling guilty. He knew stealing was wrong, but his emotions told him otherwise. When the raccoon stole cherries from the squirrel, he felt happy, and therefore in his mind, it was right and not wrong.

"I shall report you to the authorities if you do not apologize," said the squirrel. "Why must you report me for this? I have done no wrong," the raccoon responded. "It is wrong to steal," the squirrel said defiantly.

The raccoon remained silent, so the squirrel turned around to leave and report him to the authorities.

"Hey," said the raccoon. "I don't think I can let you report me." "Why not?" asked the squirrel.

The raccoon smiled and said, "If God wants me to be happy, I will do what I desire."

"It doesn't matter what you—" the squirrel tried to say, but his body was now lifeless on the ground, and the raccoon walked back home feeling he had done no wrong.

Some people argue that God wants them to be happy to justify indulging themselves in sinful behavior, but that does not make the sinful behavior righteous.

Rumpelstiltskin

by Karly Gerow

For those in the time of this, gold was a symbol of more than just wealth but of promise. A village far into the mountains, fog coating the ground creating a sticky feeling to the touch. In the distance, a kingdom bloomed with fresh royal blood and cheery coronation tunes sung as the young prince was crowned king. The villages rejoiced, praying that their new leader would bring fortune to their hungry, greedy mouths. Fresh bread with nutty crusts sat on window sills, from the poorest of folk to the richest, mouth-watering aromas graced the air.

Throughout this town, there were many an unfortunate soul. Poverty made the kindest of children swipe what meals they could find. In the grandest house, surrounded by the butcher and town apothecary, sat a man and his daughter. Not much younger than that of a young woman, she longed to venture farther into the kingdom to meet her future husband. Her father, a widower who wasted his assets on gambling and booze, convinced her to stay time and time again. Promising riches or feigning his soon demise, the girl stayed.

Finally, one day that was like any other, the man returned with his next and greatest scheme, "We should spread word of your talent, my darling. I declare you shall be known as the woman who could spin straw into gold! Once the King hears word of this surely he will ask for your hand in marriage. My very own daughter, the future Queen of Gold!" Joy radiated off the delusional old man. Though the girl desired nothing more than to be who the King loved, she couldn't help but hesitate. How they planned to deceive their ruler, she had no clue. Such clandestine meetings with her father created a wave of suspicion among the townsfolk, drawing the attention of Rumpelstiltskin.

Namb the Preamble

by Noel N. Moira

Thistledowns, soft and colorless, falling down in a graceful, nimble dance towards the Bottommost with the others on the cradling, keeping them from falling into the deep nothingness below. With a burrowing *whoosh,* a nubby head popped out from under the field of thistledown, and with another shuffle, it was able to pull itself out from under the pale fluff. As small as a thimbleful, it stood for a moment, staring at the upwards light. It wanted to see what it was, what it was like above its own birthplace, and so, the nubby wayfarer began its ascent. The wee thing didn't have a heart, nor a soul, but it wielded a silver bell on its garb, a singing warmth, the best gift and birthright the Bottommost could conjure up for its own offspring. Nimbler than the white fluff that it climbed, its gray, silvery garb that cocooned around its body twinkled as it reached the top. It couldn't speak, but inside itself its belfry bellowed faint tintinnabulations at the thistledown peak. The light shone down on the little carillonneur, its small peepholes glistening in excitement at the top of the thistledown land. It did a small, twirling, and jumping dance to celebrate its efforts, jovial at the triumph. Its barely audible jingles echoed out across the Bottommost, the thistledown field granting silent applause to the sprite's accomplishment. Its wee name was Namb.

West Coast

by Karly Gerow

My Grandma used to tell me about the West Coast. So different from where I called home, my brain collects and stores each for memory. She tells me of the blue sun, one slightly larger and grander than that of the East. Ours, tinted yellow with temperatures that could melt flesh off of bone, theirs with an eerie glow. My Grandma has never been one for ghosts and ghouls, but the second she tells of that fiery ball of chemically compounded light and warmth, a wave of reverence and unease washes over. Though I have never been fortunate enough to experience their aqua-colored crystal, I see it every night as I close my eyes. Wondering if one day I might watch the same sunrise as she.

Dear Dad,

by Karly Gerow

There's something about the way your hands
Shake.
That shakes me a little on the inside.
You can hide it under smiles and laughter
but I'm not laughing too.
I can't help but think that those tremors
Are only a fraction
of what's going on in your head.

Our family has a long history of heart problems
and anxiety,
So when you know—
when you've SEEN
—that I'm destined to the same fate as you,
Why.
Won't you tell me what caused you to be
like this flutter of a person
Never opening up,
Never trying anything scary,
Never leaving the safety of your shaky hands.

You stand tall like a mountain,
towering over others,
protecting me from the storm but bearing it ten times worse.

Even after your cup was empty,
you couldn't help but give me what little bit you could find.
Mountains hold the world and
You always hold me when I cry.
I describe you as a passive whisper in the wind
but your voice booms with heavenly grace.
Rocks make up mountains and
Mountains make up the horizon.
I wasn't lying when I said you don't fly,
you stand completely and utterly still.
Against all odds, all obstacles, all catastrophes.

I love you more than words could describe but
I don't want to live the life you do.
If ambition is stopped the second before it's started
Where will I go?
I'm not like you in the sense that I
simply CANNOT
live my life sitting and waiting.
Watching opportunity fly by but never
taking it by the hand and soaring.
I don't want my kids to worry about me the way
I worry about you.
You can't fly away from your fears.
Shaky hands don't turn into wings.

What Am I?

by Skai de Leon

Fear is a theme.

Anger is a theme.

So is happiness,

And sadness

Then what am I?

I choose to think I am happy,

But sometimes I am afraid,

A crushing weight that smothers.

And sometimes I am anger,

Hot and red like the devil.

And sadness always not far behind.

Sometimes I am all of them at once,

A fiery mix of anger fear sadness,

And at the end when it's all over?

Happiness.

Then what I am I?

Human.

About the Authors

Brendan Sack is a high school senior from North Olmsted, Ohio. He became interested in writing the summer before his junior year, and his writings have received several accolades. In 2024, he was awarded Young Writers Workshop scholarships at Messiah University and The Ohio State University learning from professional writers.

Grace Kellum is a poetry enthusiast and a high school senior. She loves reading, art, and a good cup of tea when she can get it. She enjoys writing about all manner of things, but especially the mist and vivid scenes.

Honora Quinn is a student at Mount Holyoke College and is the author of several short stories including "An Exclusive Interview With The Monster Herself" which was featured in Dreamworldgirl Zine's second issue. Additionally, she has hosted the literary podcast, *On The Shelf With Honora Quinn*, since 2023.

Karly Gerow, a ninth-grader at South Western, loves all things literary. Whether listening to music, watching movies, or doodling, she's always creating scenarios to write about. She thanks everyone for supporting her in her messy journey to becoming an author and wishes to let them know that you are loved.

Kiki Hawkins is an eighth-grade student who spends most of her time reading, watching TV, or listening to music. Her favorite types of media are horror and thrillers, which has inspired her writing style and this short story.

Lara Chamoun is a high school student from Toronto, Canada. She is the author of the forthcoming chapbook Bleeding Ghosts (Cathexis Northwest Press) and her work has appeared or is forthcoming in LIT Magazine, On the Seawall, The Shore Poetry, Barely South Review and elsewhere. She was a 2024 Adroit Summer Mentorship mentee in fiction and reads for Eucalyptus Lit.

Mabel May is a 15-year-old girl who's long life dream has been to share my crazy worlds of magic, adventure, and love. She is the author of "The Magic Keeper." But the story isn't over yet. Are you ready to dive back into Elanor?

Maura Pensinger is a high school student from Hanover, PA. She has been writing since she was six and is excited to share her work with the world. Aside from writing, Maura enjoys participating in theater and music groups and reading everything she can get her hands on.

Noel N. Moira, or Dylan Ward, is an upcoming and new novelist. He hopes to make more pieces in the near future, and he thanks the people who believed in him deeply. And finally, to the people who published his first work, he sends his gratitudes.

Skai de Leon is a merchandise creator and editor for Wild Ink Publishing. She uses her skills in art to create unique pieces that go with author book covers. Skai enjoys making crafts, reading and baking in her free time, and wants to do everything and anything--except backpack across Europe ... or swim with sharks, she's not THAT adventurous!